OLIVIA

written and illustrated by Ian Falconer

ATHENEUM BOOKS FOR YOUNG READERS
New York   London   Toronto   Sydney

Atheneum Books for Young Readers
An imprint of Simon & Schuster Children's Publishing Division
1230 Avenue of the Americas
New York, New York 10020

ATHENEUM BOOKS FOR YOUNG READERS is a registered trademark of Simon & Schuster, Inc.
For information about special discounts for bulk purchases, please contact Simon & Schuster
Special Sales at 1-866-506-1949 or business@simonandschuster.com.
The Simon & Schuster Speakers Bureau can bring authors to your live event. For more information or to book an event,
contact the Simon & Schuster Speakers Bureau at 1-866-248-3049 or visit our website at www.simonspeakers.com.

Book design by Ann Bobco
The text of this book is set in Centaur.
The illustrations are rendered in charcoal and gouache on paper.
Manufactured in China 0416 SCP
10 9 8 7 6

The Library of Congress has cataloged the original hardcover edition as follows:
Falconer, Ian.
Olivia/written and illustrated by Ian Falconer.   p.   cm.
Summary: Whether at home getting ready for the day, enjoying the beach, or at bedtime,
Olivia is a feisty pig who has too much energy for her own good.
ISBN: 978-0-689-82953-6 (hc)
[1. Pigs—Fiction. 2. Behavior—Fiction.] I. Title.   PZ7.F186501   2000   [E]—dc21   99-24003
ISBN: 978-1-4169-8034-6 (book and CD)

A detail from *Autumn Rhythm #30* by
Jackson Pollock appears on page 29.
The Metropolitan Museum of Art,
George A. Hearn Fund, 1957. (57.92)
Photograph © 1998 The Metropolitan
Museum of Art. Used courtesy of the
Pollock-Krasner Foundation/Artists
Rights Society (ARS), New York.

A detail from *Ballet Rehearsal on the Set*, 1874, by Edgar
Degas, appears on page 26. Oil on canvas, 2′1½″ × 2′8″
(65 × 81 cm), used courtesy of the Musée d'Orsay, Paris.

To the real Olivia and Ian,
and to William,
who didn't arrive in time to appear in this book.

This is Olivia.

She is good at lots of things.

She is *very* good at wearing people out.

She even wears herself out.

Olivia has a little brother named Ian.
He's always copying.

Sometimes Ian just won't leave her alone,
so Olivia has to be firm.

Olivia lives with her mother, her father, her brother, her dog, Perry,

and Edwin, the cat.

In the morning, after she gets up,
and moves the cat,

and brushes her teeth,
and combs her ears,

and moves the cat,

Olivia gets dressed.

She has to try on everything.

On sunny days, Olivia likes to go to the beach.

She feels it's important
to come prepared.

Last summer when Olivia was little,
her mother showed her how to make sand castles.

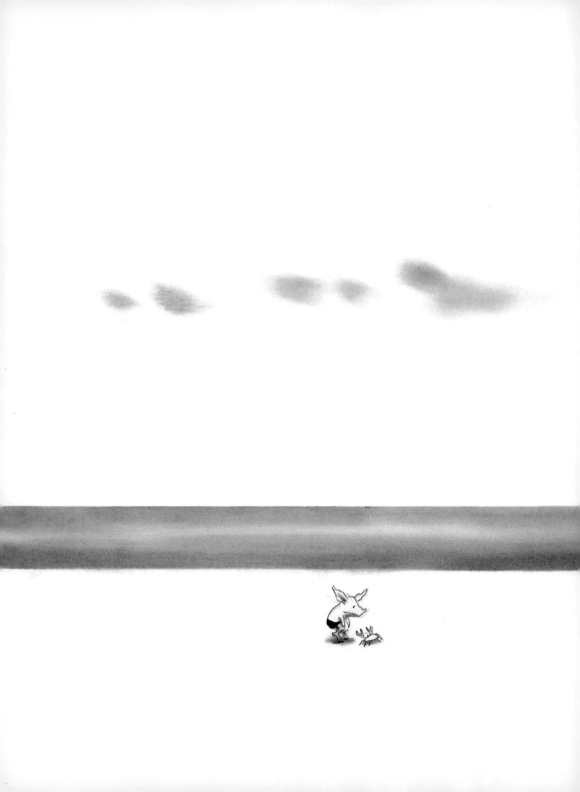

She got pretty good.

Sometimes Olivia
likes to bask in
the sun.

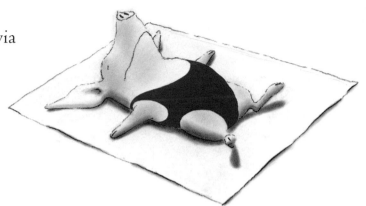

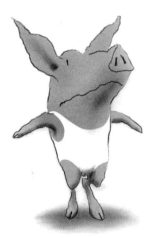

When her mother sees that she's had enough,
they go home.

Every day Olivia is supposed to take a nap.
"It's time for your you-know-what," her mother says.

Of course Olivia's not at all sleepy.

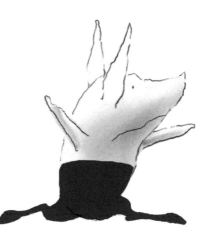

On rainy days, Olivia likes to go to the museum.

She heads straight for her favorite picture.

Olivia looks at it for a long time.
What could she be thinking?

But there is one painting Olivia just doesn't get.
"I could do that in about five minutes," she says to her mother.

As soon as she gets home she gives it a try.

Time out.

After a nice bath,

and a nice dinner,

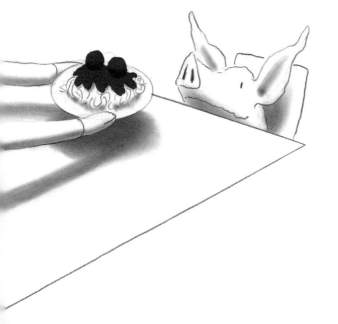

it's time for bed.

But of course Olivia's not at all sleepy.

"Only five books tonight, Mommy," she says.

"No, Olivia, just one."
"How about four?"
"Two."
"Three."
"Oh, all right, three.
But that's *it*!"

When they've finished reading, Olivia's mother gives her
a kiss and says, "You know, you really wear me out.
But I love you anyway."
And Olivia gives her a kiss back and says,
"I love you anyway too."